ANGEL
IN A
GUM TREE

Written by
Diana Chase Valerie Krantz

Illustrated by
Heather Hummel

Sandcastle

On the very first Christmas two thousand years ago, in a stable in Bethlehem, the baby Jesus was born. Since that time, each Christmas Eve, a rainbow of angels fills the heavens singing songs of love and peace.

The littlest angel sings the loudest song of all.

The other angels have chosen him to carry the joyful message right around the world.

Even to the very bottom of the earth.

Someone has whispered that Christmas in Australia is very different indeed. The littlest angel has to find out how different it really is.

He peeps into houses and sees families cooking turkeys, making puddings and wrapping presents.

He sees that Christmas brings families and friends together,
and that neighbours make sure no one is alone at Christmas time.

The angel watches children place figures of Mary, Joseph and the baby Jesus in a crib, to remember the very first Christmas.

The angel smiles to hear the old Christmas stories:

… of how all animals kneel and face Bethlehem at midnight on Christmas Eve;

… of how a cock crowed the good news to the world and a raven spread the message;

… of how a wren knitted a warm cover for the Holy Child;

… of how donkeys and oxen are specially blessed, because they shared the first Christmas in the stable in Bethlehem;

… and of how bees hummed the Hundredth Psalm — 'Make a Joyful noise unto the Lord' … hum … hum

Once more, he hears

… about the Three Wise Men who gave the very first gifts at Christmas time;

… of the Mexican boy's gift of simple weeds that changed into beautiful red flowers shaped like the Star of Bethlehem.

… and how gypsies shared their camp fire with the Holy Family as they fled from cruel King Herod.

And he reminds the robin of why all robins wear fiery feathers. Of how on that cold night long ago, his great-great-grandfather's grandfather flew between the Holy Family and a roaring fire, catching the burning sparks on his breast.

He sat with spiders as they listen to the story of how an ancestor spun a web across the entrance to a cave, to hide the Holy Family from Herod's soldiers.

Dancing lights in city streets and decorations in shop windows amaze the littlest Angel.

He wonders what gifts children will buy for their friends and families.

The angel thinks the Christmas tree is the most magical …

... the most sparkling, the most wondrous tree he has ever seen!

He watches the postman fill letter boxes with many cards and extraordinary-shaped parcels.

He sees people open letters from their families in other parts of the world.

There is mail from North America where everyone looks forward to a white Christmas.

There is news from Holland where Dutch children fill their clogs with cake and lollies for Sinter Klaas, hoping he will exchange them for toys.

BLIJDE KERSTDAGEN
from the Netherlands

YENI
YILINIZ
KUTLU
OLSUN

from Turkey

from

Greece

KALA CHRISTOULINA

A card from China reads: 'Holy Birthday Old Man'.

Sheng Tang Lap Rem

From Russia comes a card in the shape of Baboushka, an old lady who sheltered the Three Wise Kings on their way to give gifts to the baby Jesus.

SROZHDESTVOM KHRISTOVYM *from Russia*

Froehliche Weihnachten

from Italy

BUON NATALE

A letter from Germany tells how, many years ago, a man covered a fir tree with glowing candles, to show his little son how the stars looked on Christmas night.

In a parcel from Italy came a bell for the old lady Befana to ring before she climbs down the chimneys with presents for children.

The angel follows Father Christmas

to tiny outback towns,

to lonely islands

and big cities.

The angel thinks Carols by Candlelight is just heavenly!

By the time Christmas day arrives the littlest angel is quite worn out.

He checks his list.
'Glory Hallelujah,' he sings. 'Christmas in Australia
is not so very different after all.'

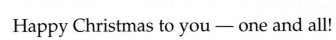

Happy Christmas to you — one and all!